Hannah's Touch

Laura Langston

orca soundings

ORCA BOOK PUBLISHERS

When nothing is sure, everything is possible.
—Margaret Drabble

Copyright © 2009 Laura Langston

Library and Archives Canada Cataloguing in Publication
Langston, Laura, 1958-
Hannah's touch / Laura Langston.

(Orca soundings)
ISBN 978-1-55469-150-0 (bound).--ISBN 978-1-55469-149-4 (pbk.)

I. Title. I. Series: Orca soundings

PS8573.A5832H35 2009   jC813'.54   C2009-902134-X

Summary: After being stung by a bee, sixteen-year-old Hannah
discovers she has the power to heal.

First published in the United States, 2009
Library of Congress Control Number: 2009926088

Orca Book Publishers gratefully acknowledges the support for
its publishing programs provided by the following agencies: the
Government of Canada through the Book Publishing Industry
Development Program and the Canada Council for the Arts, and the
Province of British Columbia through the BC Arts Council and
the Book Publishing Tax Credit.

Cover design by Teresa Bubela
Cover photography by Dreamstime

ORCA BOOK PUBLISHERS
PO Box 5626, STN. B
VICTORIA, BC CANADA
V8R 6S4

ORCA BOOK PUBLISHERS
PO Box 468
CUSTER, WA USA
98240-0468

www.orcabook.com
Printed and bound in Canada.
Printed on 100% PCW recycled paper.
12 11 10 09 • 4 3 2 1

Chapter One

A bee sting changed my life. One minute I was normal. The next minute I wasn't.

If you listen to my parents, they'll tell you I haven't been normal since my boyfriend, Logan, died. But they don't get it. When he died, a part of me went with him. Plus, I could have stopped it. The accident that killed him, I mean.

But I was normal. Until it happened.

It was the third Sunday in September, sunny and warm. School was back in. The maple leaves on Seattle's trees were curling like old, arthritic fingers. Fall was only a footstep away.

I wasn't thinking about fall that Sunday. Or school or maple leaves. For sure I wasn't thinking about bees.

I was at work, thinking about Logan, and I was cold. It was freezing in the drugstore. Bentley had the air conditioning cranked to high.

"I swear, Bentley, it's warmer outside than it is in here." We'd run out of Vitamin C, so I was restocking the middle shelf beside the pharmacy. "I don't know why you need the air conditioning on."

"It keeps the air moving." He was behind the counter, slapping the lid on a bottle of yellow pills. "Besides, fall doesn't officially start until September 23." He slid the bottle into a small white bag.

2

Like that made any difference. But Bentley, who was the pharmacist, was also the boss of Bartell Drugs. As far as he was concerned, summer was sunscreen displays and air conditioning. No matter how cold it got.

I only had to whine a few more seconds. "Take twenty," Bentley said. "It's quiet today."

I grabbed a soda from the cooler by the magazines, waved at Lila, our cashier, and wandered outside. The heat was better than any drug Bentley sold. I popped the tab on my can, took a sip, breathed in sunshine.

"Well, well, just the gal I want to see."

It was Maude O'Connell, leaning on her turquoise walker, her uni-boob and gold chains practically resting on the top bar. An unfortunate orange and blue caftan covered her plus-size body.

"My gout pills ready yet, Hannah?" she asked.

"Behind the counter and waiting, M.C." I'd called her Mrs. O'Connell only once. She preferred M.C.

Hanging from the walker was a basket lined with fake brown fur. Home to Kitty, a nearly bald ten-thousand-year-old apricot poodle (yes, Kitty is a dog) who couldn't walk. When I leaned over to scratch her head, she growled and bared the few yellow teeth she had left. I pulled back. Not from fear, but because the smell from the dog's mouth made me queasy.

"'Bout time," M.C. complained. "I called Friday, and they weren't ready."

"Friday was nuts," I said. Three-quarters of the customers at Bartell's were lonely seniors. I liked talking to them as long as they didn't bring up bodily functions.

"Your hair's growing in nice." Like Kitty, M.C. was nearly bald. She obviously missed having hair, because she always commented on mine.

"Yeah." Six months ago, I hacked off my long blond hair. After Logan died, kids I didn't even know started coming up and asking if I was "the girlfriend of the dead guy." My friends kept telling me I was different too. I didn't need the judgment or the attention. But instead of flying under the radar, I decided to *be* different. So I hacked off my hair. It was a dumb thing to do.

"The color looks nice."

It was blond, the same color it had always been. "I'm thinking of dying it midnight black next month." I played with Logan's St. Christopher medallion. I'd been wearing it since the accident. "To mark—" I stopped.

The one-year anniversary.

Everybody kept telling me I had to get over Logan; I had to move on. Like I could get *over* him. And anyway, my sadness kept him close. My sadness and his medallion—they were the only

5

things I had left. "To mark Halloween," I lied.

M.C. sniffed. "All Hallows' Eve is about more than black hair and broomsticks. It's a true pagan holiday." Her pale blue eyes took on a sudden gleam as she leaned close. "It's the time of year that spirits can most easily make contact with the living." She frowned at the look on my face. "It's true!" She grabbed my arm. "I talk to my Danny boy every year at midnight. You can talk to your Logan too."

I didn't want to talk to Logan. Getting in that car was the stupidest thing he'd ever done. The shock of his death had worn off, and I didn't cry every day anymore, but I hadn't forgiven him or me or Tom. Especially not Tom. He'd bought the beer. And insisted they race.

When I didn't answer, M.C. dropped my arm in disgust. "Okay, so you're a nonbeliever."

The truth was, I believed the dead go somewhere. It's not just lights-out, erased forever like a mistake on a test. That wouldn't be logical. In nature, everything gets recycled. Why should we be any different?

"I know you Christians." M.C. stared at Logan's St. Christopher medallion. "You've been fed a load of bull crap about All Hallows' Eve. I'm telling you, it's about as far from the devil as a daffodil."

You Christians. I thought of my friend Marie. "I'm not sure I'm Christian, M.C."

"What are you then?"

"Undecided." And before she could demand more, I changed the subject. "You'd better go get those pills before Bentley goes on his break."

"Undecided is for wusses and politicians," M.C. said as she headed for the door. "Smart people believe in something."

I walked across the parking lot to the grass on the corner. I believed in lots of things. Tennis and lululemon yoga pants. The importance of saving. Love. And God too, in a casual go-to-church-at-Christmas kind of way.

Later, after it happened, I wondered if being a go-to-church-every-Sunday kind of girl would have spared me. Then again, it might have made it worse.

I flung myself on the grass between two clumps of flowers—one orange with brown centers, the other a brilliant pink—and wedged my pop on the ground beside me. Once, this spot had been nothing but bark mulch and a few droopy shrubs. You could still see it in old pictures showing our location. But last year Bentley had removed the bark mulch, laid sod and thrown down a fistful of wildflower seeds.

For a guy who dealt drugs all day, he sure liked his flowers. Especially ones that smelled good.

The sun beat on my face. I settled with a sigh. The odd car drove up and down the street. Geese honked somewhere above me. Relaxed and finally warm, I shut my eyes.

I drifted, thinking of homework, of foods class. We'd been assigned groups to prepare theme dinners. I'd been set up with Tom, who insisted we choose Mexican because he wanted to cook with tequila. Like that would fly. Still, knowing Tom, he'd find a way to screw the rules, and we'd fail.

Tom brought thoughts of Logan.

Who was I kidding? Whenever I shut my eyes, I almost always thought of Logan.

Except, I was starting to forget the way he smelled. Don't be grossed out. Logan smelled better than anyone I'd ever known. I'd even bought a bottle of his cologne to wear. But it didn't smell the same on me as it did on him. Body chemistry, I guess.

Forcing myself to think of something else, I concentrated on the roll of earth at the small of my back, the scratch of grass beneath my palms, the warmth of the sun on my eyelids.

I floated there for a while, knowing it was almost time to go back inside. Just as I was about to sit up, I heard a slight buzz in my ear, felt a soft tickle on my cheek. I imagined it was Logan teasing me with a blade of grass. I imagined what I would do back and grew hotter still. The buzz faded; the tickling dropped to my chin.

Some kind of bug. I brushed at my face, heard an angry buzz, and then I felt it—a sharp sting on my neck.

"Ow!" The pain was intense, red-hot and scorching.

A bee sting. My first.

It had to happen sometime. And what better place to get stung than outside a drug store where I knew the pharmacist and he could pull the lid on a bottle of Calamine lotion without me paying for it.

I grabbed my soda and scrambled to my feet. Sunlight glinted off the cars passing by, the sky was an unreal pencil-crayon blue. A car horn sounded; a child laughed. The noises rushed in, filled me up.

Probably I should get the stinger out, I thought. Weren't you supposed to?

A wave of dizziness turned the world sideways. Nerves, I told myself. It was only a bee sting. No biggie.

Except the pain was spreading. Down my neck and into my chest. Sweat beaded my forehead.

Don't be silly. You're going to be fine.

I hurried toward the parking lot. The dizziness was getting worse, the noise from the cars growing louder. I knew about shock reactions; I'd learned something working at Bartell's for the last eight months. But no one in my family was allergic. To anything.

By the time I got to the parking lot, I knew I was wrong. Someone in our family was allergic to something. And that someone was me. My legs felt like they were going uphill through cement. My arms tingled, my breath was wooly in my throat.

Across the lot, I saw M.C. and her stupid Kitty dog standing in the doorway talking to Lila.

I started to run. And then everything turned black.

Chapter Two

I was going to die in the parking lot of Bartell Drugs wearing that stupid red vest and with short hair. Mom would hate burying me without my long hair.

What a stupid waste, I thought, seeing my body on the pavement. My first bee sting and it's fatal. It was almost as stupid as Logan getting in that car.

It's all part of the plan.

I felt the words rather than heard them. They became part of me. With them, I grew bigger, fuller, softer.

More accepting.

At the same time, I felt someone. Something. A warm presence.

Beside me, above me, everywhere. It filled me with a kind of hum. I wanted to look around, see who or what it was, but I didn't want to miss the scene below.

I was out of my body. I knew that. I also knew this would probably be the last time I saw myself. It was odd viewing my body from the outside. Kind of like seeing a 3-D image that looks real but isn't. The real me was up here. Strange but true. I wondered if they'd called my parents. My brother, Geoff.

It didn't really matter. Nothing did.

M.C. cradled my head. Kitty dog was in the basket beside her. Lila, the cashier, was on her cell phone.

Bentley knelt beside me and pulled something out of a package. An EpiPen.

So I *was* having an allergic reaction. I was dying. Which meant I was off the hook for that group project with Tom. And I could go find Logan and give him crap for dying.

The thought struck me funny. I began to laugh.

You must go back.

There was the voice again.

I didn't want to go back. Being here, wherever here was, was the nicest thing that had happened to me since…I don't know. Since before Nana died, when I used to stay at her house in the country, and she'd tuck me in at night and make me apple pancakes in the morning and put my hair in French braids and she would love me. This was like that love, only more.

I hadn't felt it since I was ten years old. And I didn't want to give it up.

"No," I said.

Your work is not finished.

"Someone else can pick up my shift." When I laughed a second time, I felt Logan draw near. I smelled him.

And I began to cry.

Tears ran from the eyes of the 3-D Hannah on the ground. I saw M.C. wipe them away with the sleeve of her caftan. But where I was, there were no tears, only an ache. A sweet, tender ache of a memory suddenly real. "Logan?"

He was beside me, bigger than I remembered, but invisible. The presence was still there too. I knew, somehow, that it had let Logan in. *"You can't stay,"* Logan said.

"I want to."

Something jolted the Hannah on the ground. Bentley's EpiPen had found its mark. The fuller me began to shrink and empty.

"Hannah!" Bentley's voice pulled at me. "You're going to be fine. We've called an ambulance." His hands rubbed the spot on my thigh where the EpiPen had hit.

My edges sharpened; the hum inside me started to fade. The presence was still around me. Logan too. But it was like they'd left the room.

"Go back and do it," Logan said.

"Do what?" I asked.

He said something about Tom I couldn't hear. He was starting to fade. I couldn't smell him anymore either.

"Tom's a jerk and so are you. You shouldn't have gotten into that car."

His laugh was faint but real. *"I love you too, Hannah Banana."*

Before I could answer Logan, the voice said, *Be strong.*

That voice had always been there, I realized. Inside me. Grounding me, yet moving me forward at the same time.

It was logical, and yet not. As I struggled to make sense of a truth bigger than anything else I knew, I felt a *whoosh*. Like I was being sucked backward.

And I slammed into my body.

A small crowd had gathered. I heard people whispering. Great. I hated people staring. I hated standing out. Even if I was lying down. I looked into the three sets of anxious eyes—Bentley, Lila and M.C. Four if you counted rancid Kitty dog, who peered over her basket and whined.

"Thank God," Bentley said. "I was ready to pull out a second EpiPen."

Lila squeezed my hand. "Your mom is on her way."

A siren sounded in the distance. I knew it was for me. I was cold. Even in the bright sunshine. Shivery cold.

Bentley stood. "I'll get you a blanket." I heard him ask the crowd to move on. The siren grew louder. So did Kitty's whining.

M.C. reached for her. "Hush now!" The dog's whining turned to small yips.

"She's worried about you. She wants to make sure you're okay." Before I could stop her, M.C. thrust Kitty dog in my face.

The animal flopped against my neck, a quivering mess of bald skin and bad breath. Turning away from her mouth, I awkwardly stroked her lumpy back. I was on the ground, back in my body. I was the same Hannah, and yet I wasn't. Something was different. And it wasn't just the pain in my neck or the thick wooliness of my mouth. I was, for lack of a better word, new. As if I'd been bathed from the inside out.

Be strong.

Be strong for what?

The siren was getting louder. I didn't want to go to the hospital. There was something Logan wanted me to do. Some kind of job. But the memory was going, and I needed to figure it out. I struggled to sit up. Kitty dog stuck to my neck like Velcro.

Lila gently pushed me back down. "Rest."

"She's right," M.C. said. "The medics need to look at you before you move."

Oh good. Not only was I flopped out in front of Bartell's wearing a stupid red vest that defined ugly, and with a ten-thousand-year-old rancid Kitty dog stuck to my neck, but I had to lie still and wait for a bunch of HOTTIES. And for sure they would be. The drool-worthy guys always show up when you look your worst. (And, yes, I still loved Logan, but I had my pride.)

Bentley returned with a blanket. "You're going to be fine," he said as he covered me.

I was far from fine. Clutching Kitty dog in desperation, my fingers played with the folds of her skin like she was the answer to all my problems.

She wasn't. She was the start of them. Only I didn't know it at the time.

Right then, as I felt Kitty's tiny heart beat under my hand, as I breathed in her smelly dogginess, and even with that siren growing closer, I grew calm. My shivering stopped. I became warm. Hot, even. My palms burned. I started to feel bigger again. Softer too.

Was I going back there? I shut my eyes and waited for the fullness to grow. For the hum to start. I thought about Logan and that presence. But I was too sleepy. I kept drifting off.

A minute later, or maybe five or ten, I heard the slam of doors, felt the rush of air as someone crouched beside me. A hand plucked Kitty from my neck. Chilled again, I shivered.

"Hannah?" Fingers touched my cheek. "Hannah Sinclair?"

I opened my eyes, mumbled, "Yes." A guy who looked like Jude Law smiled down at me. Damn, why couldn't these guys be ugly?

"What's your name?" Mr. Beautiful asked.

I answered, then shut my eyes. All this for a stupid bee sting. Couldn't I have gotten hit by a car, helping a runaway toddler instead?

Someone slapped a blood pressure cuff on my arm. Another set of hands probed the sting on my neck. I reached up, wanting to get Logan's medallion out of the way.

"Do you know what day it is?" the Jude Law look-alike asked.

"Yeah, it's Sun—"

"Good Lord, look!" M.C. yelled. "Kitty's walking. All by herself. Tell me I'm not seeing things?"

Sweat beaded my upper lip. I tried to sit up. Two sets of hands held me down. "Stay still," someone said.

I turned my head and saw the dog out of the corner of my eye. Kitty wasn't walking exactly, but she was standing up by herself. And wobbling forward. Twice. Which was twice more than she'd wobbled since I'd known her.

M.C. clapped her hands in delight. I paid no attention. I had something else on my mind. Logan's St. Christopher medallion. It wasn't around my neck.

"Where's my medallion?" I asked Mr. Beautiful. "Did you take it?"

"No, ma'am," he said. "You weren't wearing a medallion when we got here."

Chapter Three

They kept me in the hospital overnight for observation. Which was not smart. Hospitals are for sick people. If you aren't sick going in, you probably will be going out. But my opinion didn't count. All they cared about was that my blood pressure was super low.

All I cared about was finding Logan's St. Christopher medallion.

That and figuring out what he wanted me to do.

"Your dad and I will drive back and see if we can find it." Mom tucked in the cover on my bed. They'd finally moved me to a room after a zillion years in emergency. "Although Mrs. O'Connell promised to take another look before she went home."

I rolled my eyes. "Like she's gonna crawl around the ground by the flowers."

"I don't know. She looked pretty spry to me."

Maybe it was Mom's use of the word *spry* (I swear to God, she's the only parent since 1942 who has used the word), or maybe it was the image of M.C. dusting the ground with her uni-boob, but I started to giggle.

Mom smiled; the worry lines at the sides of her mouth disappeared. "You're going to be fine." She squeezed my arm. "They're only keeping you in for observation. It's routine."

"I know. But something happened. I went somewhere." I'd tried to tell her everything in emergency, but she'd brushed me off. I struggled again to explain the weirdness. "There was a voice. And Logan was there."

The worry creases returned. Fear darkened her blue eyes. "You mentioned that." She fussed with my pillow.

"He wants me to do something."

"He wants you to start living again." When I didn't respond, Mom added, "Maybe it's time you went back to see Dr. Fernandez."

Dr. Fernandez was the shrink my parents had insisted I see for a few months after Logan died. I didn't like her. Mostly because she started every sentence with, "What I hear you saying," and then disagreed with everything I said. Plus she had really bad teeth, and I'm sorry, but I just couldn't get past them.

"I'm not crazy." I wasn't. Was I?

"I didn't say that."

She didn't have to. Mom and Dad were worried about me. I didn't go out much. I'd lost interest in tennis. For a while, I'm sure they thought I was suicidal. But suicide wasn't the answer. Why would I leave people grieving when I knew how much it hurt missing Logan?

"We'll talk about it when you get home," she said. "I'm sure Dad's brought the car around by now." She leaned over and kissed my forehead. I caught a whiff of Mom-smell: spearmint breath mints, Ivory soap and magnolia hand cream. My eyes teared up.

"Look hard," I said. "For the medallion."

"Of course." And with one last kiss, she was gone.

Her runners squeaked as she went down the hall. I heard the ping of the elevator coming to collect her, the swish of the doors as she stepped inside. I was alone. With way too much time to think.

Had I left my body?

My practical self told me I was imagining things. My heart said I wasn't. I couldn't explain it, I didn't understand it, but I knew it as sure as I knew my street address.

The whole thing was real.

"It's not unusual to hallucinate at a time like that," the emergency doctor had told Mom. I heard her. I also heard her say it was shock. The shivering. The crying. The weird idea that I'd gone somewhere. She'd given me a pile of pills to take. Stuff to calm me down.

It wasn't working.

My senses were hyped. I swear I heard the information clerk six floors down answering the switchboard. For sure I heard the doctors at the nurses' station, the elevator moving from floor to floor, the faint *click-clack*, *thud-thud* of a machine—or was it someone walking?—down the hall.

It was M.C. She poked her head around my door and gave me a giant smile. "It's about time they sprung you from emergency."

"Did you find Logan's St. Christopher?" I tried to sit up, but my arms had gone on strike. I was so tired.

"Not yet." She pushed her walker into the room. "But it'll turn up." She wore a huge multicolored poncho over her caftan and a brilliant red beret on her head. She looked like an overweight, crazed French chef.

Disappointed, I flopped back down.

"Hold on, I'll hoist your bed." With a speed that surprised me, M.C. wedged her walker into the small space between my bed and table, leaned over and flicked a switch. The head of the bed rose.

The movement caught the attention of Kitty dog, who appeared from under the poncho and launched herself at my face, wiggling and yipping and licking my chin like she was my new best friend. I hadn't seen the dog move this much in...well...never. She pretty much always acted her age—ten thousand years old.

"You're not supposed to have dogs in here." Kitty moved to my ear, which was way better than having her anywhere near my nose.

"What they don't know won't hurt them," M.C. said.

The dog was moving down my neck toward my sting. I grabbed her snout and held it between my hands, trying to stop her and keep her quiet at the same time. She snarled and showed

her teeth through my fingers. "Okay,
okay." I let her go. She threw herself
at my other ear.

"I can't stay long." M.C. began
pulling things out from under her
caftan a tub, a soupspoon, a metal
thermos top. "But I wanted to come
and thank you." She poured something
thick and orange into the thermos lid.
I smelled onions and spice. My stomach
growled. "It's not every day someone
heals my Kitty dog."

What was she talking about? I hadn't
healed the dog. The dog was probably
too ashamed to walk, but the sound of
the ambulance had scared her. (If you
were a dog named Kitty, would you want
to walk?)

Before I could point this out, M.C.
thrust the mug into my hand. "Carrot-
ginger soup," she said. "After all
you've been through, you need the
grounding energy."

So what if she didn't make sense. I hadn't eaten since lunch, and it had to be almost nine o'clock. One of the nurses had promised to bring me a sandwich, but that was hours ago. The soup was hot and tasty. M.C. had claimed to be a good cook over the last few months, but I figured she was bragging.

She wasn't.

After downing a second cup, I leaned back on my pillow and asked the question I needed answered. "What do you mean, all I've been through?"

"Lifting off and getting the power and coming back and healing Kitty."

A shiver ran down my spine. "Lifting off?"

"Your body might have been lying in Bartell's parking lot, but after telling me that you'd been stung by a bee, you left. You were gonzo." Her pale blue eyes glittered as she stared at me. "You took yourself off to the great beyond, where you got yourself the power to heal Kitty." She gestured to the dog. "Look at her. She's walking."

No, she wasn't. My new best friend was sitting on my knee, drooling.

"I did not heal her." If I had, I would have given her hair. And cured her bad breath.

"Yes, you did. You healed her with the laying on of your hands."

She had to be kidding.

"It's true," she insisted.

M.C. had been watching *Heroes* too much. Either that or the gout medicine was getting to her. "That only happens on TV, M.C. This is real life."

"Of course, it's real life." She thrust the thermos lid at Kitty, who slurped so loudly I was sure the nurse would hear it and think I was having a seizure. "It's a real miracle, is what it is. Miracles happen, ya know. And not just on the Miracle Network either."

I snorted. "Yeah, they happen in comic books too."

M.C. opened her mouth to speak, but the *slap-slap* of a nurse's shoes out in the hall stopped her. She grabbed Kitty and stuffed her under the poncho. "Listen to me, young lady. You're a healer now. It's nothing to joke about. Hear me?"

"Visiting hours are over," a smiling nurse said from the doorway.

"I was just leaving." M.C. picked up the thermos lid and the last of the soup. She leaned close and whispered in my ear. "You've been given a gift, Hannah. Use it wisely." M.C. was wrong. She was messed up. A total whack job. She'd named her dog Kitty. Anybody who did that couldn't be trusted.

So why was there a part of me that wondered?

Chapter Four

I was back in school on Tuesday. Not that I had to go. Mom suggested I rest for another day. I think she wanted to get me in to see Dr. Fernandez.

I didn't want to see Dr. Bad Teeth, and resting wasn't easy. Not after M.C.'s announcement that I was a healer like Jesus Christ himself. Next she'd be telling me I could turn water into wine and asking for samples.

Foods was first block. When I got to class, Ms. Drummond was frantically throwing ingredients into all the cooking stations.

I slid onto the stool beside Marie. "What's going on? I thought we were figuring out the menus for our theme dinners today."

"There's been a change in plans," Marie said.

Drummond was always changing things. Which might work in my favor, since I was determined to get her to switch me out of Tom's group.

Marie stopped doodling on her wrist and gave me the once-over. "You look like crap."

"Tell me something I don't know." I hadn't slept well, thinking about M.C.'s comment and worrying about Logan's missing medallion. And when I finally dozed off, a dream of Logan woke me.

He wanted me to do something, and I couldn't figure out what. I was tired. Even extra makeup couldn't hide the bags under my eyes.

"I can't believe you landed in the hospital because of a bee sting." Marie stared at me. "What really happened?"

For a second, I almost told her. But after Logan died and I started questioning God, Marie decided my soul needed saving, and she kept hounding me to see her parish priest. If I told her I felt a presence *and* a voice *and* Logan, she'd have the guy calling *me*.

Not that I was passing judgment. But still. My dad was a lapsed Catholic who had no time for religion, and my mother believed everybody—Christians, Buddhists, even our neighbor who worshipped some star in the next galaxy and believed silver UFOS would take us all there when the world ended.

No wonder I had commitment issues.

"Hannah?"

I mumbled something about allergies and overprotective parents.

Ms. Drummond clapped her hands. "Listen up!" When the talking faded, she continued. "Today you'll break into your dinner groups and I'll walk you through a simple recipe for a shake."

Marie leaned close. "Kristen, Lexi and I made an amazing shake with Coffee Crisp ice cream, chocolate powder and a whole lot of vodka Saturday night. Kind of like a Frappuccino, only better. You should have been there."

No thanks. I felt lonely with my friends, especially when everybody was having fun. They always made it a Really Big Deal when I didn't drink. I hated being singled out. Besides, how could I party with Logan lying in the ground?

"I want to see you work together before we finalize the groups," Drummond said. "After that, we'll get you started developing menus."

This sounded good. Tom and I did not work well together. Even a blind toad could see that.

"The usual rules apply," Ms. Drummond added. "Clean hands, aprons, long hair tied back. The ingredients are in your stations. Look them over and get ready for my demonstration."

I slid from the stool and headed for the back of the room. Marie fell into step beside me. "A bunch of us are grabbing pizza at lunch," she said. "Why don't you come?"

"Maybe."

She frowned. Marie knew "maybe" meant "no."

When I walked into the only cooking station large enough to take a wheelchair, Tom peered at me over his sunglasses. Logan would never wear sunglasses again. I bit down hard on my lip. Because Tom had goaded him into that car.

"Hey, Hannah Banana," Tom said.

Beside him, Alan Kim laughed and fiddled with one of the chef's knives.

"Don't call me that." Never mind that Tom had coined the phrase first. It belonged to Logan.

"Lighten up," Marie murmured.

Ignoring them both, I checked the counter to see what we had. There was vanilla yogurt, milk, juice and a selection of fruits: bananas, blackberries, pears. "Looks like your basic fruit shake," I said.

Tom grinned. "I've got a way to make that special." He flipped open his jean jacket. I saw a small bottle of Malibu rum. Marie snickered.

Alan whistled. "Nice work, Shields." He picked up a second knife, juggled the two of them clumsily.

"Don't even think about it," I said.

"You never used to be such a priss," Tom challenged. "Not way back when."

I felt the flush creep into my cheeks. A long time ago (before I developed a brain), I'd dated Tom Shields (gag me). In fact, he'd introduced me to Logan. He hadn't been so bad back then. A little bit out there, but mostly okay. We'd gotten along.

Not now. Every time I looked at Tom, the pain of Logan's death hit me again. Tom had gotten off with a sore leg. Muscle damage, he said. I wasn't so sure. Half the time he was in his wheelchair, half the time he was on crutches. I figured he used both for effect.

"Still playing with balls?" he teased.

Alan almost dropped a knife. I didn't bother replying. Tennis was my thing; I'd come close to making the USTA junior team last summer.

"I hear doubles is the way to go." Tom's eyebrows danced up and down his forehead.

Alan hooted. The knives clattered to the floor. "Shit, Shields, now look." One of the knives had hit his thumb on the way down. "Shit, shit, double shit."

Drummond was talking to a group at the back. But she was going to notice any minute. Especially with the blood dripping onto Alan's jeans.

Alan grabbed a towel, wrapped it around his thumb. Within minutes, the blood seeped through.

"You might need stitches," I said. "We have to tell Drummond."

"No." He was whiter than the milk on the counter. I wondered if he'd severed an artery. Did thumbs have arteries? "You know what a tight-ass Drummond is about knives. I'll be kicked out of class and my dad will string me up." Alan jerked his head to the towel. Blood was dripping to the floor. "Do something!"

I grabbed a clean towel from the counter and removed the soiled one. My breakfast waffle flipped in my stomach. Talk about ugly. The tip of Alan's thumb was hanging by a string of skin.

I slapped the clean towel on before anyone could see. "Get Drummond!" I squeezed Alan's thumb, applied as much pressure as I dared. "He needs a doctor."

Then I felt it. The same buildup I'd felt after the bee sting. Only this time it happened quickly, like a movie on fast forward. And this time I didn't pass out.

The voices of my classmates faded; the color of the fruits on the counter blurred. Suddenly the presence was there. Making me bigger, fuller, softer.

And warm. Especially on the palms of my hands.

The moment became an hour, and the hour turned into a day. Time hummed, stretching up and out, wrapping itself around me, around Alan's thumb. I felt grand yet small. Love-filled. Perfect. I knew Alan was perfect too.

I heard Drummond's voice off in the distance. "What's going on?"

Tom said something about the knife slipping. Marie added that the gash was ugly and deep. As soon as they spoke, the hum started to fade. The *whoosh* tugged at me.

"Let's see." Drummond reached for the towel.

The instant she touched us, it all stopped. Time snapped into its small self, like an elastic returning to size. The presence left. So did the hum.

As Drummond unwrapped the cloth, I knew exactly what she would find. A cut, for sure, but no stringy bits, no hanging thumb. I started to shiver.

"You must have thick blood," Ms. Drummond said, staring at the gash. "The bleeding's already stopped. But we still need to get it looked at."

After Drummond took him away, Marie and I wiped the counters. Or Marie did. Suddenly I was so tired I could hardly stand. "That was *major*," she said.

"It wasn't that bad." I didn't want to think about what it meant if it was that bad.

Tom wheeled over with more paper towels. "Are you frickin' blind?" He stared at me so intently I wanted to squirm. "That was a slice and dice. Alan's thumb was practically off. And then it wasn't. It was totally weird."

Weird was right. Even weirder was the fact that my palms were still hot.

I didn't want to think about what that meant.

Chapter Five

Alan's slice and dice totally freaked me out. Something had happened in that foods room. I'd felt it. Did that mean I was a healer like M.C. said? No way. I was as normal as a slice of cheddar and just as boring.

Then why was all this stuff happening?

News of Alan's accident spread quickly. By the time I got through English, I had five text messages from people wanting details, including a note from Marie reminding me about lunch.

That was so not on my "to do" list. I didn't want to hear any more about Alan, and I was too tired to talk. Thinking fresh air might perk me up, I switched off my phone and headed for Bartell's. I wanted to look for Logan's St. Christopher. Maybe even talk to Bentley about bee stings.

The sky was overcast. The air was still but warm. The walk cleared my head, calmed me down. By the time I turned the corner and came face-to-face with the spot where I'd been stung, I was feeling better. I knew there had to be a logical explanation for everything.

And I knew Logan's medallion was somewhere in the grass too.

The scent of flowers was heady. A lone bee buzzed through the bright pink blooms. I tensed and stepped back. When it finally moved on, I dropped down and searched the ground. I even gave the flowers a quick shake, thinking maybe the medallion was stuck between some stems. It wasn't.

Disappointed, I headed across the parking lot, my gaze settling on the spot where *it* had happened. Where I'd left my body and talked to Logan.

There was an SUV parked there. I stood beside it for a minute, wanting to understand. Hoping Logan or the presence would come back so I could ask some questions. Nothing.

Inside the drugstore, Lila was beside the cash register, filing her nails. "Anybody turn in Logan's St. Christopher medallion?" Mom had put up a missing sign, but it didn't hurt to ask.

"Not that I know of, but Bentley would know for sure." She stopped mid-file and squinted at me. "Aren't you supposed to be in school?"

"It's lunchtime." I headed for the pharmacy.

Bentley was just finishing up with a customer. As she left, I sidled up to the counter and gave him a little wave.

"What are you doing here?" He clicked his pen and slid it into the pocket of his white lab coat. "Don't you have classes today?"

"It's lunch." Why did every adult think they were the school police? At least Bentley was a parent. Lila was just nosy. "I thought I'd stop by and see if anybody turned in Logan's medallion."

"Not yet. Sorry." He peered at me over his gold-rimmed glasses. "Nice to see you up and around. You gave us quite a scare."

"Yeah." I hesitated, not sure how to put into words what I wanted to ask.

"I'm wondering, do people ever have long-term reactions from bee stings?"

He began straightening the cough medicine display on the counter. "Occasionally people who are sensitive to stings become more sensitive. If that's the case, your doctor can give you something to carry with you."

"But nothing else?" I asked.

"In rare cases, it can take people a full twenty-four hours to react to a sting, but that's about it." Satisfied that the cough medicines were in line, he looked at me. "What else were you thinking of?"

Serious, crazy, superpower effects. "I don't know. Like maybe it rewires their brain or something?"

He chuckled. "I don't think so."

I tried again. "Or maybe they get electric tingles, or feel full in their head, or spaced out or..." My voice trailed off. "Or something."

"I've never heard of it," Bentley said.

I felt a wet tongue poking into my ankle. I looked down. *Kitty dog?*

The phone rang behind the counter. Bentley turned to answer it. "But if you're not feeling one hundred percent, go back to your doctor."

I heard the familiar *click-clack, thud thud* of a walker hitting the tile floor. "Hannah!" M.C. called. "Just the person I want to see."

Kitty raced around me in circles, leaping and jumping and whimpering for attention before she started bathing my other ankle. My stomach flip-flopped. The change in the dog was nothing short of a miracle. She was acting like a six-month-old puppy. I liked her better when she was ten thousand years old and stuck in her basket.

M.C. shuffled over, her uni-boob heaving under her flowing purple top.

"I'm glad I caught you." She took my elbow with a firmness that surprised me. "I came in to leave an envelope, but now you can take it with you. Let's go outside."

Kitty dog bounced out the door ahead of us. She was sprouting hair on her bald spots. I narrowed my eyes. Did Kitty have a twin? Was this some kind of joke? But then I almost stepped on Kitty dog's tail. She bared what was left of her teeth, and I caught the reek and knew it was the same dog.

M.C. bent down and picked her up. "She's like a teenager again." Kitty squirmed so much she had to put her back down. "You gave her her life back."

My heart was doing hip-hop in my chest. If I had done that to Kitty, it meant I had done something to Alan, which meant my normal-as-cheddar life wasn't so normal anymore.

"I didn't do anything."

"You did. I told you in the hospital. You have the power now."

M.C. was padded-walls crazy. Kitty dog barked at a crack in the sidewalk. So was her dog. "People don't change from a bee sting," I said. "The world doesn't work that way."

M.C. retrieved a beige envelope from the basket on her walker. "And you know this how?"

I didn't answer.

"Here." She thrust the envelope into my hand. "This is stuff I've been saving from magazines and newspapers. I even went online and printed a few things out." I must have looked surprised, because M.C. added, "Not everybody over seventy is useless where the Internet is concerned." She gestured. "Have a look."

The envelope was crammed with bits and pieces: articles on faith healing and something called Reiki. Information on a group of healers in the mountains of Peru. A *TIME* magazine feature on physics.

"That one explains everything." M.C. pointed to the physics article. "It's really interesting."

I doubted it. Physics was about as interesting as my left toenail, only way more confusing.

"Thanks," I said as I turned to go.

"My phone number's there too," she called after me. "In case you want to call me."

No way did I want to call her, I thought as I headed across the parking lot. There was enough weirdness in my life already. I didn't need more.

I didn't go back to school. Instead I went to the library and searched the shelves for something that might help me understand what was going on.

The Complete Idiot's Guide to Spiritual Healing was fairly detailed. I spent the next couple of hours reading about everything from massage and magnets to crystals, voodoo, positive thinking and prayer.

All of a sudden I was thinking positively and praying to a God I'd never really thought much about before: *Please, God, make me normal. I am normal, right, God? I am. My life is not a comic book, it is cheddar-cheese normal and please, God, keep it that way.*

By the time I got home that afternoon, Alan was the star of Facebook. Ten friends had updated their status and were talking about him. There was even a picture. He'd put it up himself, with the tagline, "Look, Ma, no stitches."

Great.

I updated my note about Logan's missing medallion and went back to reading about Alan.

The more I read, the more I felt the dry heaves coming on. My friends had no idea what had happened, only that something strange and wonderful had. Strange, maybe. Wonderful, no. A bloodfest might not have done Alan any good, but it would have made me feel better.

Bounce wandered into the bedroom and meowed for attention. I picked her up to give her a cuddle. As I turned back to the computer, the chat icon popped up. It was Tom.

Gag me.

Sinclair, I need ur help with the car wash. U promised.

My breath caught. I'd promised to help *Logan* with a pile of things, including the car wash that kicked off this year's fundraising. Logan, not Tom.

U there?

Here, I typed back, stalling for time.

We're doing the signs Thursday at noon, Tom added. *Car wash is this Sunday.*

Just before he died, Logan had talked about chairing the fundraising committee for senior year. He'd been stoked. Determined to raise enough money to get us a kick-ass year-end camping trip. He was pretty much guaranteed the chair spot. Tom got it instead and vowed to do the job in Logan's memory.

U coming?

Was this what Logan wanted me to do? Help Tom with the car wash? I'd pretty much decided to skip it, since Tom would be in charge.

I thought of what Logan had said when I'd gotten stung: *Go do it*. And he'd mentioned Tom too. I remembered that much.

Okay, my fingers typed before I could stop them. *I'll help.*

A car wash was simple stuff. If that's all Logan wanted, I could deal.

Obviously I was lying to myself. Because that night I had the worst nightmare ever.

Chapter Six

It woke my parents. And when they came in to see why I was screaming, I apparently grabbed Dad around the neck and practically choked him as I yelled, "Put out the fire!"

I don't remember that part; I was still asleep. But Dad told me in the kitchen the next morning, right before he said I needed to go see Dr. Bad Teeth.

"It's almost a year since Logan died." He was pouring coffee into his stainless-steel travel mug. "And you're still struggling. You need to see her again."

What I needed was some of that coffee. My eyes were barely open. Half the cat food I'd poured into Bounce's dish had ended up on the floor, and she was making slow, delicate work of cleaning up my mess.

"Especially considering the added stress of the last few days," Dad added.

He had no idea. I hadn't told them any of it: not about M.C. or Alan's thumb. Not even much about my dream. M.C. was in it. So was Logan. I was wearing his St. Christopher medallion, except it was choking me. I kept trying to get it off, only the presence was there telling me to be strong. I was gasping and gasping for breath, and then I burst into flames and floated away. It was a total creepfest.

"I'll have Janice make the appointment." Janice was Dad's secretary. He grabbed his keys from the counter and dropped a kiss on top of my head. "She'll call you."

I grabbed a muffin from the fridge and listened to his footsteps echo down the back steps. Great. Like I needed Dr. Bad Teeth making me feel worse.

Bounce meowed. I opened the back door to let her out. She'd been on my chest when I'd woken up this morning. Mom must have put her there after my nightmare. The cat was so old she couldn't jump anymore.

Bounce wasn't limping.

A chunk of muffin caught in my throat. No way. I peered down the stairs, watched her walk to the pond for a drink. Bounce had limped since getting hit by that car three years ago.

She had to be limping. I stared harder. She *wasn't* limping. At least not much.

A chill snaked its way down my back. There had to be a logical explanation. For everything. Maybe my imagination was working overtime. Maybe I was going crazy. Either way, I was going back to Dr. Bad Teeth.

That afternoon, I sat across from Dr. Fernandez while she read my file, wiggling in her oversized leather chair, trying to get comfortable. I hoped this visit would help me figure things out.

"Your parents told me a little of what's happening," Dr. Fernandez said when she looked up. "But I'd like to hear it from you."

Focusing on the mole beside her eye instead of those ugly yellow horse teeth, I told her about Logan's missing medallion. "It's like losing him all over again," I admitted.

"That must be difficult."

Uh, yeah. "I guess I should have checked the clasp before I started wearing it. It was probably loose."

Her square black glasses slid down her nose. She pushed them back up. "You feel guilty."

It was a statement, not a question. I nodded.

"And would you call that real guilt or fake guilt?"

According to Dr. Bad Teeth, real guilt came from deliberately doing something wrong. Fake guilt was beating yourself up for something you had nothing to do with.

I shrugged. "Fake, I guess." Fake or real, it didn't bring Logan's medallion back.

"And what about Logan's accident?" she asked. "Do you still feel guilty about that?"

Of course I did. But Dr. Bad Teeth thought that was totally fake guilt.

"Like you said, I didn't give him the key and put him behind the wheel." I was repeating what she wanted to hear. "He did that himself."

She studied me from behind her thick glasses. "Have you truly accepted that, Hannah?"

I hadn't. I'd watched that race. I was there. That made me responsible. They'd told us since preschool that the bystander was as responsible for the bullying as the bully. This was the same thing.

The corners of her mouth turned down. My silence told her everything she needed to know. "You did the best you could," she reminded me. I wondered if she was sad about my feelings or sad that her therapy hadn't worked. "You asked him not to race."

I did, at the party. Except I hadn't been forceful enough. I could have pitched a fit. But I didn't want to make a scene. I didn't want to spoil everyone's fun. And now Logan was gone.

"You need to let the guilt go," she said.

Letting go was hard for me.

"Guilt can do terrible things to a person."

It was the opening I needed. "I've been having nightmares and..." I hesitated. If I told her about the presence and the power and Bounce, she'd fill me full of pills and lock me up with the crazies. I didn't belong there. On the other hand, I needed to figure out what was happening. "Dizzy spells and stuff." It was as far as I would go.

"I'm not surprised. Unresolved guilt causes stress, and stress causes many reactions."

"Really?"

"Absolutely. And the one-year anniversary just adds to it."

Relief turned my bones liquid.

M.C. was wrong. I wasn't a healer. I was stressed. Big time. Thank you, God.

"I understand you think Logan is telling you something?" she said.

"Yeah. When I was stung, it was like I heard his voice." I waited for alarm to flash across her face, but it stayed blank. "It's like there's something he wants me to do."

Now she'll pick up the phone, I thought. And the men in those white coats will come and take me away. But she just looked at me and said, "I think if Logan wants you to do anything at all, Hannah, he wants you to let go. Let go of your guilt, let go of him and move on."

The visit with Fernandez made me feel a little better, although when I got home that afternoon, the worry returned. Bounce had caught a mouse. She'd left it in the hall. She hadn't done that in years.

Something was definitely up with her. At dinner, I asked my parents if they'd noticed Bounce was more active.

"It's the glorious fall weather," Mom said. "Everybody's feeling better. Even cats."

That was it, I decided. Mom was right.

Thursday morning, when I walked into the tech-ed room at eight o'clock ready to make the signs for the car wash, I was feeling normal. No more nightmares, no more weird happenings. It was all stress. Already I felt better.

The group was assembling spray paint and cardboard at the back of the room. "Where's Tom?"

"Late," Brad said. "Mornings are rough for him. It takes him a while to get moving."

It took me a while to get moving some mornings too. But I didn't bail on people when they were counting on me.

We laid the cardboard out on the work tables. "When his ankle broke, they fixed it with a steel plate and a pile of pins," Brad added as we began stenciling in words. "But his body keeps trying to reject them."

Something close to sympathy curled around my heart. I tamped it down. Tom had wanted to race. So what if he had a sore leg? He was still alive. I'd take a sore leg for the rest of my life if I could have Logan back.

By foods class, Tom was back.

"So whatcha think, Thumbs?" he said to Alan as I slid onto a stool beside Marie. "Wanna try juggling three knives today?"

"No way," Alan said with a grin. "One more accident and I'm out. My dad will kill me if that happens."

Before I could stop myself, I was gazing at the spot where I'd held that towel on Alan's thumb. The area was clean, blood-free. No sign of what had happened. Yet I felt uneasy just glancing in that direction.

To cover my confusion, I pulled Mom's Mexican cookbook from my binder. "I thought we could use this to plan our menu." I opened it; Marie peered over my shoulder.

"We don't need a book," Alan said. "All we need are corn chips, salsa and tequila!"

"Good plan, my man!" The two guys high-fived.

"You guys do the appetizers and beverages then." As soon as Drummond caught a whiff of the booze, they'd be booted. And I wouldn't have to work with Tom after all. "We'll do the entrée and dessert."

We settled on guacamole and fresh salsa with chips, chicken enchiladas and a simple flan for dessert. While the guys goofed off, Marie and I drew up the grocery list.

"And who is doing what?" Ms. Drummond asked when she stopped by our table.

"Hannah and I are doing the entrée and dessert," Marie said as Drummond scanned our list. "The guys are doing the appetizer and beverage."

Ms. Drummond frowned. "I don't think so."

She didn't want the guys working together. No doubt because of Alan's accident.

"Alan and Marie will do the beverage and dessert," she said. "Tom and Hannah can do the entrée and appetizer." The muffin I'd choked down at breakfast almost came back up. Before I could open my mouth to argue, she was gone.

Tom smirked. "Glad I've got you on my team, Hannah Banana. I know you're good with a towel. But are you any good with a knife?"

Being in Tom's group was bad enough. Being paired with him would never work. "I'm going to talk to her." I slid from my stool.

"And whatcha gonna tell her?" Tom taunted. "That you'd rather partner with Logan?" He snorted. "Well, lucky for Logan, he's dead and he doesn't have to deal with any of this shit anymore."

Lucky? I whirled around. "That's a disgusting thing to say. If you hadn't dared him to race, Logan would still be alive." I grabbed Marie's arm. "Come on. Let's go talk to Drummond."

Chapter Seven

Drummond wouldn't budge. I had to work with Tom Shields. "The past is past," she said when I reminded her about Logan's accident. "It's time to move on."

Friday we did our dry run. I let Tom do the guacamole because I figured he couldn't mess it up. Wrong. He turned it purple. And he burned the enchiladas when I wasn't looking too. I had to test everything again at home that night.

Saturday I worked a full shift at Bartell's. Late in the day, a woman called and said she'd found a St. Christopher medallion nearby. Bentley let me leave early. I raced to her house, only to find the medallion was round. Logan's was oval.

My disappointment burned.

Sunday, the day of the car wash, dawned clear and warm. As we pulled into the Shell on Thirtieth, I thought of Logan. We'd gassed up here a month or so before he died. It had been sunny and warm that day too.

"We'll come back later to get the car washed," Mom said as she helped me unload the signs and flags. We weren't starting until ten, but half a dozen kids were already there. Not Tom though.

Figures, I thought.

After the manager of the car wash told us where to set up, I took over, dividing people into teams: a lather-and-scrub team, a rinse team, a publicity team. The publicity people took the flags and poster boards and headed for the corner. The rest of us began assembling supplies and filling buckets.

Tom didn't show up until 10:30. By then, we had a lineup six deep, including an SUV so dirty I wondered how the driver could see out the windshield. Tom was in his chair today. Good excuse not to do much, I thought, watching him wheel through the sudsy puddles. Unkind, yeah, but I was wet, cranky and tired of watching Tom play the victim. Logan was the real victim.

"Brad has his brother's car, and he's taking a bunch of us to Alki Beach later," Marie said when I brought a fresh bucket of water to the lather-and-scrub side. She was using her dad's fancy handheld scrubbing wand. "We don't have many nice days left. Why don't you come?"

Because Alki Beach meant booze, and I wasn't interested.

"I have…" I hesitated. "Plans."

Marie knew I was lying. "Come on, Hannah, don't be such a wuss!" She whirled around fast, wand in hand, hitting Lexi right in the face. Hard.

"Ow!" Lexi yelped. She fell to her knees and cradled her face.

I knelt beside her, put my hands around her shoulders. "Are you okay? Let's see."

White-faced, Marie crouched on her other side. "I'm sorry, Lex. I didn't know you were there."

Lexi's nose had taken the worst of it, I realized. It was red and swollen, starting to bleed. Automatically, I reached out to wipe the blood away.

As soon as I touched her nose, it happened. The presence swept through me like a tidal wave, filling and stretching me until I couldn't tell where I stopped and it started. A car door slammed in the distance. Light glinted, diamond-bright, off the chrome of a motorcycle. I hardly noticed.

Time slid sideways. I grew softer, warmer. My hands began to burn.

No.

I couldn't do this again. I wouldn't. I dropped my hands so suddenly Lexi almost fell sideways.

And that's when I heard the voice. *Be strong,* it said.

It was my turn to almost fall over. I was hearing voices now? Oh no. No, no, *no*. "I'll get the first-aid kit." I mumbled.

Marie glared as I walked away. It didn't matter. Nothing did. Because I wasn't cheddar-cheese normal anymore. And I had to leave before anybody else found out.

I went to see M.C. I'd dropped a prescription in her mailbox once on my way home, so I knew where she lived. And since she'd told me about the power in the first place, I figured she could tell me how to get rid of it.

"You're looking all hot and bothered," M.C. said after she opened the door. I followed her down the hall. My legs felt like they weighed a million pounds. I was afraid if I sat down, I'd be too tired get back up. "What's gotten under your skin?"

"Something happened at the car wash today." Kitty dog pranced ahead of us—and I mean pranced. The thought that I was somehow responsible for the dog's rebirth did not make my heart sing.

"What?"

I stared around her kitchen. The place was cluttered with books and papers, bowls of fruit, dirty dishes. I moved some newspapers and sank onto the chair. I told her about Alan, about Bounce, about Lexi. About the rush of power, the presence, the way time stretched every time I touched someone who was hurting.

"It sounds pretty normal to me." M.C. said as she filled the kettle. "Considering."

Considering that I was a complete freak. Nice.

M.C. threw two tea bags into a cracked floral teapot and sat down. Her uni-boob rested on the table. I tried hard not to look. "How do I know it's real?" I still couldn't bring myself to use the word *healer*.

"What makes you think it's not?"

"Maybe I'm imagining it." I stifled a yawn. It was like I hadn't slept in a thousand years. "I can't see it or prove it."

"The wind is real, but we can't see it. We only see it moving the leaves on the trees. Maybe this is God's way of moving the leaves for you."

God moving my leaves? Yeah, right. "I'm not five years old here, M.C." I wanted to lash out, to tell her this whole thing was stupid. That *she* was stupid. She'd been there from the beginning. She'd told me I was a healer. I wanted to make this her problem, not mine. Except it wasn't. I stuffed my anger down and said, "A bee sting and now I'm a healer? It doesn't make sense."

"There are a million things in the world that don't make sense, a million things we don't understand. That doesn't make them any less real."

The kettle whistled. M.C. got up to make the tea.

"The doctor says I'm stressed. It could be that."

"Maybe," M.C. said as she plopped the floral pot on the table between us. "And maybe it's a gift."

"A gift?" At the sound of my raised voice, Kitty dog growled and bared her teeth. "This isn't a *gift*. It's a curse." M.C. selected two ivory cups from the counter and wiped them with the sleeve of her caftan. "That's a little dramatic, don't you think?"

Her matter-of-fact tone pissed me off. "Easy for you to say." Heat crept up my neck. "Your life hasn't suddenly gone sideways." Kitty growled at my tone again. "Seriously, just tell me how to get rid of it. Or do I have to spend the rest of my life not touching anyone?"

She poured the tea. "You're asking the wrong question."

"What do you mean?"

"Instead of asking how to get rid of it, you should be asking what it is you're supposed to do with it. How you're supposed to use it."

"I don't want to use it."

M.C.'s pale blue eyes sharpened. "Most people aren't in the habit of handing back gifts."

I was silent.

"You know what your problem is?" M.C. didn't wait for me to answer. "You're too rigid. You won't bend. You need to learn to roll with life's punches, take the good with the bad. You need to accept things as they come." She stared hard at me. "And let things go when it's time."

I knew she was talking about Logan and his medallion as much as she was talking about the healing thing. And I so didn't need it. "I have to go." I was too tired for this. Coming here hadn't made me feel better; it made me feel worse. Maybe I should go back to Fernandez. Or talk to Mom.

Or maybe I should keep my mouth shut and my hands to myself for the rest of my life.

"We don't always get what we want," M.C. said as she walked me down the hall to the door. "Sometimes we get what we need."

Chapter Eight

All my life I'd hated being different, I'd hated standing out. Now I was freakoid different. If there was any doubt in my mind, it flew out the window when I got home after my talk with M.C.

Bounce had caught a robin. It was fluttering around the drapes when I stopped in the doorway of the dining room.

"Get the broom," Mom ordered as the bird flew into the wall. She grabbed a chair, kicked off her heels and went into chase mode.

Eventually we got the bird out the window. Bounce, who sat in the corner watching while we chased it, was on the windowsill meowing the minute we set it free.

"You stay inside!" Mom scolded as she set the broom in the corner. She collapsed into a chair, straightened her skirt and wiped her forehead. "I'll need to touch up my makeup." She wore her best sweater set, and there was a wrapped bouquet of daisies on the table. My parents were obviously going out.

"Bounce isn't limping anymore," I said. "She's jumping onto my bed again. She's hunting. She's acting like a kitten."

"I've noticed."

I heard Dad banging around upstairs. In a few minutes he'd come down and say it was time to leave. "Do you think it's possible for people to heal animals?"

"Anything's possible." Mom reached for the flowers, straightened the bow. "Why?"

"Bounce has been sleeping on my ankles since I got stung by that bee. Maybe I healed her."

"Oh, sweethcart." A wistful expression turned her face soft. "Bounce is seventeen. She's old. I know you don't want to face it, but she's not going to be around for many more years."

I jumped in with both feet. "M.C. thinks I'm a healer."

Mom looked startled. "What?"

The sound of Dad's voice floated down the stairs. "Hey, Barb, have you seen my brown sweater?"

"Hanging behind the bedroom door," Mom called. She turned back to me, an indulgent smile on her face. "M.C. is a funny old woman."

Funny wasn't the half of it. "Seriously. I told you. Something happened to me when I got stung by that bee. I went somewhere. I talked to someone. M.C. thinks I have healing powers now."

"You heard the doctor in emergency. Your reaction was severe. You were imagining things."

"But what if I wasn't? What if it's real?"

Worry turned her blue eyes stormy. She looked down at her shoes, slid them on. When she glanced back up, her eyes were calm. She gave me her fake "everything's fine" smile. "Then Bounce is one lucky cat, isn't she?"

I wasn't sure who to talk to next. Dad maybe? Mom again? To make matters worse, Sunday I had another nightmare. I didn't burst into flames or float away, but Logan was there, insisting I had something to do. Only his voice was so garbled, I couldn't understand a single word. Obviously helping with the car wash wasn't it.

"We need to talk," Marie said in homeroom Monday morning. "Meet me at lunch."

I could tell she was upset. Probably because I'd bailed halfway through the car wash. I dozed through English, struggled through geography, and by the time I met Marie in the cafeteria at noon, I had my story down: I'd left early because of cramps.

Perfect solution.

Marie made small talk about her science project as we loaded up our trays and headed to a table by the window. Nobody joined us. Marie had obviously warned them off.

She popped the lid on her tomato soup. "Why did you run off on Sunday?"

"Cramps." I unwrapped my ham-and-cheese sandwich. "Really bad ones," I added for the extra sympathy factor.

She rolled her cracker packet between her fingers, ripped it open and tipped the crumbs into the soup. "Lexi said she felt a jolt when you touched her."

A lump of bread and ham lodged itself into the back of my throat, a perfect plug for my airwaves. It was almost a minute before my coughing stopped. "What's she talking about?" I upended my bottle of water and chugged.

"She felt something weird," Marie said as she studied me. "An electrical current or something."

Heat warmed my cheeks. I felt self-conscious, like everybody in the cafeteria was staring. "Of course she felt something. She'd just had her nose bashed in by a heavy-duty steel wand."

My hand was shaking as I picked up my sandwich. "How is she anyway?"

"She'll be okay," Marie said. "She's lucky her nose wasn't broken."

I didn't respond.

"Lexi said when you stopped touching her, the jolt went away." Marie scooped up some soup. "It totally freaked her out."

I could have cracked a joke or laughed it off. And if M.C. had been more helpful, or if my mother had been more understanding, maybe I would have. But I was confused. I didn't know who else to talk to. Marie believed in God. She believed in the power of Jesus and his love. That presence—whatever it was—was a powerful kind of love.

I dipped my toe in the pond of truth. "Maybe it was...I don't know...healing power in my hands or something."

Marie started to laugh. "You're kidding, right?"

"No."

"As in, *you* made Lexi better?"

"Why not?" I felt my heart race. "Healing is real. Lots of churches believe in it." I repeated what I'd learned on Wikipedia.

"Don't be such a tool."

I wanted her to believe me. "Alan, remember?"

"Yeah, right." She laughed a second time. When I didn't say anything, a look of discomfort flitted across her face. "Quit goofing around."

"I'm not." I wanted her help figuring this thing out, but it was so strange and so unbelievable I knew I had to start small. "When I held that towel over Alan's thumb and when I touched Lexi's nose, I felt..." I hesitated. "I dunno. Something big and powerful."

Her eyes widened. She leaned forward. "What was it?"

I picked at my sandwich crust. "I think it's healing ability."

"Only God does that. Through the Holy Spirit."

"Didn't Jesus heal people?"

Marie stared at me for a minute. She picked up her spoon, dunked it in her soup. "Jesus was the son of God."

"Okay."

Marie said nothing. She just kept staring and stirring.

"What about the rest of us?" I demanded. "You told me once we're all sons and daughters of God."

She glanced around the cafeteria before looking back at me. "That's different," she murmured quietly.

"How?"

"It just is."

I was angry at how easily she dismissed me, furious with my parents for not giving me any kind of church education. "The Bible is full of miracles," I said. "Maybe that's what this is. A miracle." Bounce's recovery was a miracle. For sure. But there was no way I was bringing the cat up.

Marie paled and glanced away again. The nearby tables were full, but nobody was paying us any attention. "Only Jesus can perform miracles," she whispered. "Are you saying Jesus is working through you?"

I started to tell her more about the presence, but I stopped. How could I explain something I didn't understand? One thing I did know, though, the presence was bigger than any one person. "No," I said.

The color drained from her face. "If it's not from Jesus, it's evil. It's of the devil."

I didn't believe in the devil. And how could a presence that was so love-filled be evil?

Marie began loading her food back on her tray: soup, cracker wrapper, milk, cookie. "You've been weird since Logan died, Hannah. But you're really losing it now."

"I am not!" A part of me worried that she was right. Another part of me knew I was normal.

"You need help," Marie added.

My stomach clenched. How *dare* she? "And you're two-faced."

Her eyes widened. "Excuse me?"

It amazed me sometimes how Marie juggled two completely different sets of friends—the school/party crowd and the youth group/church crowd. "You sit there judging me and talking about Jesus, and yet you're out every weekend partying and drinking. You have this so-called church life, but I don't see you living it."

"God doesn't mind if we have a good time."

"So it's okay to get pissed, but it's not okay to heal someone?" I snorted.

"Either that's a convenient excuse, or God has screwed-up priorities."

Poppy red spots of color flared in her cheeks. "And either you're playing with evil, or you're imagining things." She stood and picked up her tray. "I just hope it's your imagination." And without a backward glance, she walked away.

Chapter Nine

I faked the sniffles. Since my colds often turned into chest infections, it was easy convincing Mom to let me stay home for a couple of days. I snuck to the library and checked out more books—one on healing and another on psychic stuff—but mostly I surfed the Net. Okay, mostly I worried.

I shouldn't have told Marie anything. I should have cracked a joke and brushed her off. I just hoped she'd keep her mouth shut.

Accepting the fact that I couldn't spend the rest of my life in my bedroom, I went back to school the day of our theme dinner.

When I walked into foods, the ovens were preheating and the room smelled faintly of cinnamon. The spicy warmth made the place feel cozy. Lexi stood in the middle of the room, surrounded by people. Scratch cozy. Clutching my bag of groceries, I headed for our cooking station.

"Hey, can you believe it?" Lexi called out as I walked past.

Oh no. Had Marie told what I'd said?

I kept on going. "Believe what?"

"Mandy Kloss is pregnant."

I was grateful that they weren't talking about me, and also grateful that

I was the first of our group to arrive. At least I had two things to be grateful for, I thought as I unpacked my groceries. Because I sure wasn't looking forward to working with Tom. And seeing Marie wouldn't be a thrillfest either.

"Hey."

Speak of the devil. Or should I say, the saint? Marie even looked the part this morning in her pale pink sweater. "Hey," I answered. She was staring at me with the strangest expression on her face.

Well, wasn't this awkward? I turned back to the counter, rearranged the chicken and peppers, the tortilla wraps, the cheese.

"How are you feeling?" she asked.

The tone in her voice got to me, like, I don't know, chalk on the board, a needle in my skin, an insult. Obviously she thought I was crazy.

I whirled around. "I'm *fine*."

Tom and Alan walked into the class and stopped to talk to Lexi. Knowing I only had a minute, I asked, "Who did you tell? About what I said the other day?"

She turned fifty shades of red.

Oh God. So much for Mandy Kloss. "Who?" I demanded.

"My pastor," she whispered. "He wants to see you."

And let someone else tell me I was the Devil's BFF? No thanks. "Anybody else?" I pressed.

"No!"

It suddenly occurred to me that if Marie had told, the whole religion thing would have come up, and that was a subject she usually avoided. In fact, I think the only people at school who knew about her church life were me and Kristen. Plus, Marie didn't gossip. Not usually.

"Pastor Rick is a really good guy," she added.

I didn't need her pastor judging me or making me more afraid than I already was. I needed help figuring out what was happening. And what I could do about it.

She pressed a slip of paper into my hand. "Call him."

I stared into Marie's warm brown eyes. She was just trying to help. Even if it wasn't the kind of help I needed. I shoved the paper into my pocket. "Thanks."

Alan swaggered into the cooking station and plopped his bag onto the counter. Bottles clunked. "I've got everything we need for the sangria," he said.

Tom's crutches thudded softly against the floor as he hobbled to Alan's side. "For the *virgin* sangria," he said. The two of them broke out laughing and started shoving each other sideways to get at the bag.

If Alan and Tom brought booze, I was going straight to Drummond. I glanced at Marie. She was chewing her lip; she knew how I felt. Barely breathing, I watched them unload the ingredients: purple grape juice, apple and lemon juices, club soda, some oranges. No booze in sight. I started breathing again.

Smirking, Tom leaned against the counter. "So, Hannah Banana, what can I do for you today?"

The suggestive tone in his voice set my teeth on edge. But if we started arguing, we'd lose marks, and there was no way I'd let that happen. Ninety minutes, I repeated to myself. Ninety minutes and I'm free.

I grabbed an onion, slapped it down in front of him, along with a cutting board and knife. "Peel and cut," I ordered. If he was going to be an ass, I'd give him the nasty jobs.

"I'll peel your onion any day."

Alan snickered.

Pretending not to hear, I reached under the counter for the grater. "I'll grate the cheese."

"Cheese, please," Alan said. The two guys laughed like they were watching a special on the Comedy Network.

I had the cheese grated in less than a minute. I set it aside, oiled a pan and glanced over at Tom. I wanted to brown the onion along with the green pepper and chicken. But the way he was goofing off with Alan, he was going to be a while. He'd put his crutches down, and he was having trouble standing. "Why don't you sit at the table and cut," I suggested, surprised by the jolt of pity I felt.

He glanced at me. There was an odd, pinched look on his face. "Sitting is for wusses," he said.

Whatever. I washed and chopped the pepper, opened the package of tortilla wraps, greased the casserole dish.

"Your onion," Tom said when he set the cutting board on the counter beside me a few minutes later. He was bobbing all over the place like a sailboat in a storm.

What a hack job, I thought. The pieces were way too big; I was going to have to cut them again.

"Problem?" Tom asked.

I glanced up, prepared to lie, and that's when I smelled it. Booze. Something must have shown on my face, because Tom's smirk deepened. "Have another job for me, Hannah Banana?"

"You've been drinking."

"Sssh." Tom shot a look to the front of the room, where Drummond was talking to a couple of other kids.

Startled, Marie looked up from the flan crust she was rolling. Alan bolted to my side.

"It's not even *nine thirty* in the morning," I said.

"You got a problem with that?" he asked.

"I've got a problem with *you*." My anger boiled up, dark and heavy, choking my air, erasing all thoughts but one: Tom's drinking had killed Logan. How dare he walk in here drunk and remind me of that?

I poked him with my finger. "You're an asshole, Tom Shields. A selfish prick. You don't think of anyone but yourself. Ever. You only do what you want. Party hearty, that's your motto, right? Well, that motto killed Logan, and if you keep it up, it's going to kill you." There was a blank, unreadable look on his face, and it inflamed me. I poked him again, harder this time.

"Don't touch me," he snarled. His face filled with color. "You have no right."

"And you have no right to walk in here drunk and ruin it for the rest of us.

Now get out of my way." I shoved past him harder than I needed to.

He pitched sideways. Automatically, I reached out and grabbed his arm to stop the fall. As soon as I touched him, it happened. My anger surged, bringing the power with it. It rose and filled me, stretching me beyond the class, beyond the school, back to the size I'd been after the bee sting. I felt Logan. I felt the presence. I felt the hum.

And I knew what I was supposed to do. I knew why the weirdness was happening, and I knew what Logan wanted. I knew my purpose.

I was supposed to heal Tom Shields.

No freakin' way.

I dropped my hand, let him go. The heat and power and fullness raced out of me so fast I felt cold and empty and small.

And when Tom fell to the floor, I turned and walked away.

Chapter Ten

Cruel? I don't think so.

The guy was drunk. I didn't want to help him. Besides, as far as I could tell, the only help Tom needed was somebody to tie his hands behind his back so he wouldn't drink so much.

I didn't realize until later how sick he was.

"Apparently the pain in his leg has been getting worse for weeks, and he's been self-medicating with booze," Marie said when she called that night. I was sitting in my window seat with Bounce on my lap and the radio playing softly in the background. "His mom kept trying to get him to the doctor, but he wouldn't go. Turns out he's got some kind of raging infection around the steel pins. They've got him on IV antibiotics. According to his sister's MySpace page, he could lose his leg."

"That sucks." It did. I was still choked that Tom had come to foods drunk, and I'd never forgive him for daring Logan to race, but losing a leg was ugly. Shame wormed through me. I shouldn't have shoved him.

Help Tom.

Logan was inside my head.

"I wonder if I should go see him." I didn't want to. I still had trouble believing that I could heal people, that healing existed at all. And for sure I didn't want to heal Tom Shields.

"Me and Lexi might go see him tomorrow afternoon but, um, I think his family would, you know, rather it was just the two of us."

There was an awkward pause. Marie didn't want me there. *I* didn't want me there.

She changed the subject. "I'm praying for him," she said. "You can too. Anybody can do that."

Even me. Somebody who didn't go to church. Somebody who heard voices, who felt a presence, who thought her dead boyfriend was sending her messages.

"Right."

"Did you call Pastor Rick?"

"Not yet."

Another awkward pause. Then Marie said, "By the way, Drummond says we can do the meal over next week, just the three of us." I heard a familiar song drift out from the radio. "And we won't lose any marks," she added.

"That's good."

It was Van Morrison singing "I'll Be Your Lover Too." I stopped breathing. How random was that?

"For sure," Marie said. "It's one thing to be grateful for in this whole mess."

Grateful. I clicked off and tossed the phone down beside me. The familiar lyrics filled my bedroom. *"I come…to be the one…who's always standing next to you."* My eyes blurred; a lump the size of Manhattan closed my throat.

It was our song. Logan's and mine. We hadn't picked it (trust me, we would have picked something better), it picked us. It followed us around and kept popping up everywhere we went. The only reason we noticed was that our fathers both loved Van Morrison.

I buried my face in the pillow and began to weep. "*Yes, I will*," Van Morrison sang. "*Yes, I will.*"

"No, I won't!" I lifted my head and yelled at the wall. "I *won't.*"

How dare Logan ask me to help the guy who had raced with him?

I wouldn't. I couldn't. And I would go to the hospital and prove it.

I didn't want to go during visiting hours and risk running into Marie or Lexi, so I went about 10:30 the next morning.

Hospital routines were predictable. There was always a lull after 10:00, once breakfast was over and the doctors had done their rounds. Get in, prove a point, get out. That was my plan.

I walked in the front door like I belonged and headed straight for the elevator. Luck was on my side; nobody stopped me. Following the directions Tom's sister had e-mailed, I got off the elevator and turned left. It wasn't like I'd get lost. I knew the floor; I'd stayed here after my bee sting.

When I saw the three nurses at the desk, my heart skipped a beat. I needed to get past them without being stopped. I turned my head and looked the other way. Silly, but I was playing that little kid game: if I don't see them, they won't see me.

Three steps past. Then four. And five. A nurse cleared her throat. I was going to get busted. I just knew it. But I didn't. Fifteen seconds later, I was around the corner and home free.

Tom was halfway down the hall, in a semi-private room. I hesitated in the doorway. There was an empty space where the other bed was supposed to be. At least I didn't have to worry about another patient complaining that I was breaking the rules. But Tom's mom was there, sitting curled over him like a comma. I should have expected it, but I hadn't. I must have made a sound, or maybe she sensed me, because she looked up.

"You're Hannah Sinclair," she said when she came to the door. We'd met at Logan's funeral, but I hardly recognized her. The last eleven months had not been kind. Her face was heavily lined, her hair in need of a cut and color.

"Yes. I'm—" *I'm here to see your son so he can verbally abuse me and I can prove to my dead boyfriend that he doesn't want my help.* "I thought I'd stop in and say hi. Just for a minute."

"He's not really up for talking," she said. "He's had a rough night."

I tried, Logan. I did.

"But if you don't mind sitting with him, I'd appreciate a chance to grab a cup of coffee and a muffin from downstairs," she said. "I can't eat in front of him. The smell of food makes him sick."

"Sure." I followed her to the bed.

She leaned down and whispered something in Tom's ear. Then she straightened and took her purse from the back of the chair. "I won't be long." Her footsteps echoed out the door.

I slid into her seat. Tom's eyes were shut. He was on his back, still and white. Was he even breathing? Nervously I studied his chest, feeling a flutter of relief when I saw the rise and fall of the sheet. Starting to second-guess myself (what was I supposed to do now—wake him up and say Logan wanted me to give him a healing?) I glanced around the room. It was standard-issue hospital: a bathroom in the corner, a wall-mounted TV, and machines. Machines hooked up to Tom.

One had a screen with a spiky green line, the other held a bag of clear fluid.

"What are you doing here?" He spoke so quietly at first I thought I'd imagined it. But when I glanced back, his eyes were open. He was staring straight at me.

"I...um..." *Should I tell him the truth? Should I pick up his hand? Yeah, that would so fly.* "I had an errand to run. I thought I'd come in and say hi."

"Done. Now leave." He closed his eyes again.

I couldn't. I'd promised his mom I'd wait until she came back.

"Go," he said.

I bit my tongue. *Be kind. The guy's sick.*

"I don't need you sitting there judging me for being a screwup. Now go."

"I'm not judging you."

His eyes flew open. "You are."

I didn't respond.

"I don't need you beating me up. I can beat myself up."

Yeah, right. If Tom had a conscience, I'd never seen it. More tongue-biting.

"Don't you believe me? Don't you think I'm sorry?"

No. My tongue was probably bleeding by now.

He fisted the hospital blanket in his hand. "I have a real bad infection."

Here was my chance to tell him. I opened my mouth, but he spoke before I could.

"I could lose my leg. They're deciding tomorrow."

My control broke. "You're worried about your *leg?* Logan's dead. I bet he'd trade you places."

"You think I don't know that?" His voice climbed. Moisture pooled in the corner of his eyes. "I can't forget. I never will! Logan was my best friend. If it wasn't for me, he'd still be—"

His face crumbled. He rolled over and faced the wall. "Get out of here."

Oh, crap. His anger was one thing, but I hadn't expected him to cry.

His shoulders shook. Tears mangled his words. "Just go!" Great gulping sobs filled the room.

He was crying the way I'd cried for months after Logan's death. My old pain yawned open, a great black hole that threatened to suck me in.

Blinking back tears, I rushed to shut the door. I didn't want the nurse to hear. I prayed his mom would take her time too.

"Logan wouldn't want this," I said, sitting back down.

His answering wail was haunting; it curled the hair on the back of my neck. "Tom!" I reached out but stopped just short of touching him. I was afraid to. "Tom, don't."

He kept crying.

After a minute, I couldn't stand it. There was only one way to comfort him. Taking a deep breath, I reached out and touched his shoulder.

Chapter Eleven

I was taking a chance. If Lexi felt something when I touched her, Tom might too. But I couldn't let fear stand in the way of being kind. Touching Tom felt right and natural. Since the accident, there'd been moments when my grief for Logan had almost choked me. Sometimes I'd been alone with it. Other times Mom had been there, stroking my hair, soothing me with her touch.

Tom deserved the same comfort. "I know you're hurting." I rubbed his bony shoulder through the sheet. "I know you feel bad. I do. But it'll get better. It will."

I braced myself for the hum, for the stretch, for the presence. A part of me wanted it to come, and bring Logan with it, and a part of me wanted it to stay away forever so I could be normal again.

But all I felt was Tom's misery, the guilt that needled him with every breath. His leg wasn't the only thing hurting. The pain of Logan's death was like a black mark on his soul.

He blamed himself. I saw that now.

He'd been hiding his feelings behind a mask of indifference and cruelty. That's probably why he drank so much. To try and forget. It was working so well for him too. Not.

After a minute, his crying slowed. I kept my hand on his shoulder and willed the presence to come. For the first time, I wanted it to come. I *wanted* Tom well.

But my body was as empty as a glass waiting for milk.

It wasn't going to work. M.C. was wrong. Marie was right. I had imagined everything. So what was it Logan was trying to tell me? Why was I here?

Tom shifted under the covers. I lifted my hand and leaned back in my chair. He rolled over, stared up at the ceiling. He was probably dead with embarrassment. I would have been. *Dead with embarrassment.* The irony of the phrase didn't escape me.

"Marie and Lexi will probably come by this afternoon." I wanted to pretend the last five minutes hadn't happened.

He was silent.

"Everybody's worried about you."

He turned his head. His cheeks were streaked with tears, his eyes too bright. Fever, I thought. "I owe you an apology," he said.

I owed Tom an apology more. I *had* been judging him. I'd blamed him for Logan's death. Anger wouldn't bring Logan back. Neither would guilt. Dr. Fernandez was right: guilt was a waste of time.

"I've been a total jerk to you since it happened."

"I've said some awful things too." I didn't want to talk about the accident anymore. For the first time in a year, I was ready to look forward and not back. "Can't we try and forget?"

He gave a tiny smile. "Friends?" He propped himself on an elbow and held out his hand.

That's when I knew. *This* was what Logan had wanted. For Tom and me to be friends. For us to forgive ourselves and let go of our guilt. Fernandez had been right about that too.

"Friends." I took his hand and squeezed. It wasn't the kind of healing I'd come here to offer, but forgiveness had to count for something. If nothing else, I felt lighter and happier than I had in almost a year.

Then, just as I was about to let go, a million pinpricks exploded inside my body. Suddenly I was alive in a way I'd never been alive before.

A part of me sat on the chair holding Tom's hand, but the other me—the fuller, softer me—grew and stretched and rode the hum. And I wasn't alone. The loving presence was with me.

Tom's voice floated out like a distant wind. "What's happening?" I felt him tug his hand away.

But I wouldn't let it go. "It's okay," I said.

I knew it was. Even though I didn't

understand, I knew this was right and real and nothing to be scared of. The knowledge brought a powerful heat that rocked my body and shot out my hands.

"I feel weird," he said.

Of course he felt weird. He was sick.

"All tingly," he added. "Like there's an electric charge running through me."

He felt it, just like Lexi. But Tom wouldn't keep quiet about it. He'd tell people. For sure.

The thought made me dizzy with fear. I might be able to laugh it off or put it down to him being sick, but somebody was bound to figure it out. Tom himself might connect the dots: Alan, Lexi, then him. Or Marie might spill. What if my friends figured out how different I really was?

Be strong, the voice said. *Don't be afraid.*

I knew if my fear grew any bigger, the *whoosh* would snap me back to the smaller me. And it would all be over.

I could drop Tom's hand and stop this now. Fly under the radar for the rest of my life. Work to make this healing thing go away. But Tom would lose his leg.

If I helped him, I risked standing out and being different. And who knew where that road would lead? Other people were bound to think like Marie. Other people were bound to think I was crazy. I'd hate that.

"Help him."

It was Logan. He was here. I smelled him. Tears clogged the back of my throat as I stared wildly around the room. Where was he? I wanted to see him again. Just once more.

"What's going on?" Tom asked as he balanced awkwardly on his elbow. His pale face reflected fear and confusion and guilt.

His guilt was going to be with him a long time, I thought, staring into his feverish eyes. Losing his leg wouldn't make it go away. And whether he lost his leg or kept it, I knew he'd remember the accident for the rest of his life.

That kind of hell seemed a lot worse than any kind of hell I might face. I couldn't control what people thought of me. All I could control was me. And this.

I had to help Tom. I pushed my fear away. There was a tickle at the back of my neck, a soft puff of air by my ear.

"Thank you."

And then Logan was gone. The presence, however, grew stronger.

I was vaguely aware of Tom lying back on the bed, of me scooting close so I could continue holding his hand. He complained some more about heat and tingling. I can't remember what I said—I was mostly thinking about Logan—but I must have said something funny, because Tom laughed a little, called me Hannah Banana, and then he shut his eyes.

I don't know how long we sat like that. Time didn't make sense. I was getting okay with things not making sense.

Until his mom came back, and I left the room. That's when the last thing happened. And that's when I started to wonder if maybe I really was losing my mind.

Chapter Twelve

As I headed for the elevator, I felt like I could sleep for a thousand years. I was exhausted. Way more tired than I had been after Alan's thumb. After touching Lexi's nose. A nurse disappeared into a room up ahead. A pink-coated lab tech pushing a needle cart gave me a curious look as she walked by.

So what if I got stopped now, I thought. So what?

But when it happened, I was annoyed.

"Excuse me, miss?" I was four steps past the nurses' station, in clear sight of the elevator. I needed sleep. I hardly had the energy to push the elevator button, never mind drive home. I'd have to put the air-conditioning on high and blast it in my face to stay awake.

"Miss!" The voice rang out again. I stopped, reluctantly. "Visiting hours don't start until noon."

"I didn't know," I fibbed as I turned around. "But I'm leaving now."

"Oh. It's you." It was the same freckle-faced nurse who had looked after me the night of the bee sting. She smiled. "I can't believe it. Your timing is perfect."

I guess that depended on your point of view.

"I meant to call last week, but I got busy and then I was off five days. Hold on a minute," she said. "I'll be right back."

I watched her go into a small glassed-in office behind the station. She bent over a desk, rooted through a drawer. Hurry up, I thought, yawning.

Seconds later, she was back. "Someone left this for you." She held out her palm.

I couldn't believe it. It was Logan's medallion. For sure it was his. Right down to the tiny chip on the upper left corner.

"I'm sorry it took so long, but like I said, I was off for a week. Calling you was on my 'to do' list for today." She laughed. "And here you are." She dropped the medallion into my outstretched hand.

My fingers folded around it. I'd get the clasp checked, I thought, clutching it to my chest. Replaced even. Relief made me giddy, light-headed. "Was it the ambulance guy?" They'd probably found it on the ground when they'd moved me to the stretcher. Maybe it slipped off when I fainted. "Did he turn it in?"

"No." The nurse shook her head. "A young man dropped it off. About your age. He had black, black hair."

It couldn't be. I started to tremble.

"Are you sure it wasn't the ambulance guy?" My voice came out in a squeak.

"Oh, I'm sure." She chuckled. "None of our attendants have dimples like that."

Logan. I turned to instant Jell-O. My knees were shaking so much I could hardly stand up. It didn't make sense. It wasn't possible. I was insane to even think it.

But Logan's St. Christopher medallion pressed into my palm.

There are a million things we don't understand, M.C. had said. *But it doesn't make them any less real.*

"I asked if he wanted to leave a message," the nurse added, "but he said no. He seemed to be in a hurry."

In a hurry. A half-laugh, half-cry bubbled up my throat. "Yeah." I reached up to put the medallion on. There was nothing wrong with the clasp. I knew that for sure.

"Let me help," the nurse said, coming out from behind the desk. I felt her cool fingers against the nape of my neck. Had Logan touched her, I wondered. Had he *really* been here? Did it even matter? "There."

The medallion settled on my skin like a soft kiss. "Thanks." I fought back tears and rubbed the small silver disk between my fingers. Everybody said I had to let Logan go, even M.C. Learn to accept and learn to let go, she'd said. But this...I brought the medallion to my lips. Maybe one day I'd be ready to let it go. To take it off and drop it into a jewelry box, but not now. Not yet. Letting go of my grief was enough of a job.

The nurse studied me with the practiced eye of a health-care professional. "You're awfully pale," she said. "Are you all right?"

"I'm fine."

More than fine, I thought as I walked to the elevator. While I waited for it to come, I gazed at the bulletin board.

There was a notice for yoga classes Thursday at noon. A picture of a white cat with the words *free kittens* written beside a phone number. And there was a car poster. It was a red car, some fancy thing Logan would have recognized. Above it, in bold black letters, were three words: **Live life large**.

There was a soft *ping* and the *swish* of doors as the elevator opened. I walked inside and pushed *M* for main.

Live large. I thought of what had happened in that room with Tom and how he'd be okay now. That was large. I thought about how large I felt when I touched someone who was hurting. I thought about the hum, the presence, that feeling of love.

Life *was* large, I thought as the elevator bumped to a stop. Only most of us lived it small. Most of us couldn't see the truth, even when it burned the palms of our hands.

The doors slid open. Not anymore, I thought as I reached up and touched Logan's St. Christopher. Not anymore.

Laura Langston is the author of *Exit Point* in the Orca Soundings series, along with teen novels and picturebooks. Laura lives in Victoria, British Columbia.

Also by Laura Langston:

CCBC Starred Our Choice
PSLA Top Forty

Exit Point
978-1-55143-505-3 PB
RL 2.8